This book is dedicated to my adorable dad, age
ninety-three, who read me Beginner Books
when I was little.

Copyright © 2020 by Molly Coxe

All rights reserved. Published in the United States by Random House Children's Books,
a division of Penguin Random House LLC, New York.

Random House and the colophon and Beginner Books and colophon are registered trademarks
of Penguin Random House LLC. The Cat in the Hat logo ® and © Dr. Seuss Enterprises, L.P.
1957, renewed 1986. All rights reserved.

Visit us on the Web!
rhcbooks.com

Educators and librarians, for a variety of teaching tools, visit us at RHTeachersLibrarians.com

Library of Congress Cataloging-in-Publication Data is available upon request.
ISBN 978-0-525-64546-7 (trade) — ISBN 978-0-525-64547-4 (lib. bdg.)
ISBN 978-0-525-64548-1 (ebook)

MANUFACTURED IN CHINA
10 9 8 7 6 5 4 3 2 1
First Edition

A Ticket for Cricket

by Molly Coxe

BEGINNER BOOKS®
A Division of Random House

Little Cricket
likes to hop.
Hop!

Little Cricket likes to snap.

Snap!

Little Cricket likes to tap.

Tap!

"Look!" says Little Cricket.
"I can hop, snap, and tap!"

"Stop!" say Mom and Dad.

"Baby Cricket needs to nap."

Little Cricket likes to chirp.
Chirp! Chirp! Chirp! CHIRP!

"Listen!" says Little Cricket.

"Listen to me chirp!"

"Shhhh," say Mom and Dad.
"Baby Cricket needs to burp."

Little Cricket can't
hop, snap, tap, or chirp.
What can he do?

"I know," says Little Cricket.

"I'll go somewhere new!"

Little Cricket
buys a ticket
for a trip—

on a rocket ship!

The rocket zooms
to Planet One.
Planet One looks really fun.

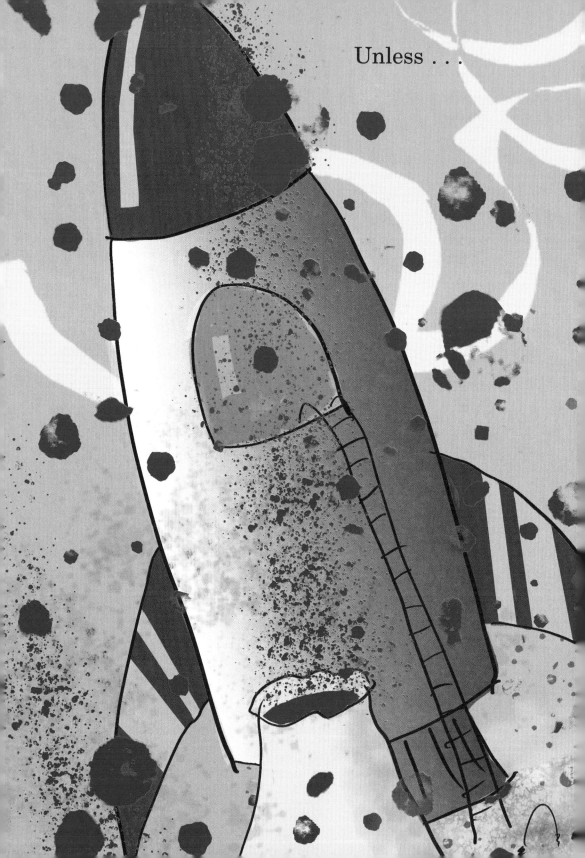

Unless . . .

Uh-oh! Maybe not!
Planet One is REALLY hot!

The rocket zooms
to Planet Two.

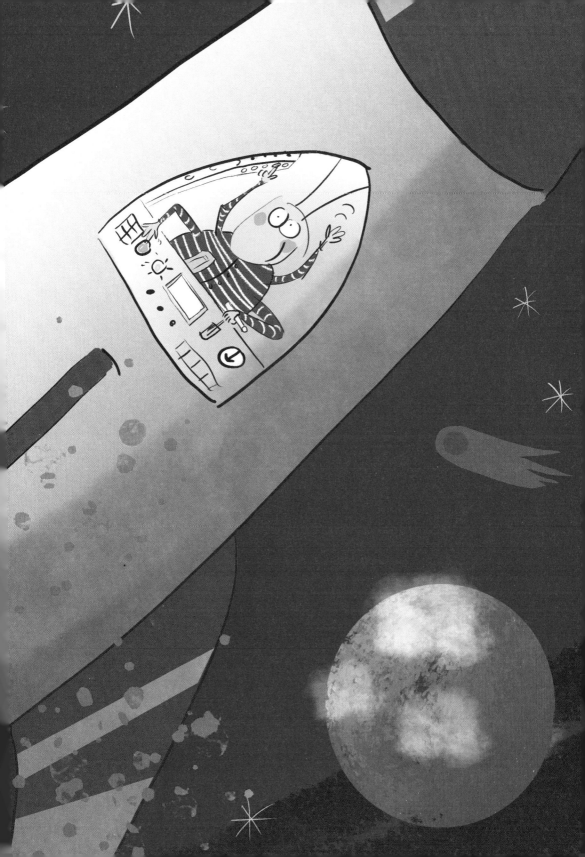

Planet Two is very blue.
And super cool! And really nice!
Unless . . .

It's ice!

The rocket zooms to Planet Three.

It has a giant golden tree!

It also has small gals and guys
exactly Little Cricket's size.

They like to hop, snap, and tap!

They're lots of fun and never nap!

Life on Planet Three is tops!

Unless . . .

The tree is not a tree.

It's not! It's not!

IT'S NOT A TREE!

Little Cricket waves his ticket.
Will anybody see?

Someone sees!
It's Mom and Dad.
Little Cricket is home.
He's very glad.

"We love you, Little Cricket,"
say Mom and Dad.
Hop! Snap! Tap! Chirp!